PUFFIN BOOKS

SUPER SIDE KICKS

PUFFIN BOOKS

UK | USA | Canada | Ireland | Australia
India | New Zealand | South Africa

Puffin Books is part of the Penguin Random House group of companies
whose addresses can be found at global.penguinrandomhouse.com.

www.penguin.co.uk
www.puffin.co.uk
www.ladybird.co.uk

First published in Australia by Penguin Random House Australia Pty Ltd 2019
Published in Great Britain by Puffin Books 2020

002

Copyright © Gavin Aung Than, 2019

The moral right of the author has been asserted

Cover and internal design by Gavin Aung Than and Benjamin Fairclough
© Penguin Random House Australia Pty Ltd

Printed and bound in Great Britain by Clays Ltd, Elcograf S.p.A

A CIP catalogue record for this book is available from the British Library

ISBN: 978-0-241-43485-7

All correspondence to:
Puffin Books
Penguin Random House Children's
80 Strand, London WC2R 0RL

GAVIN AUNG THAN

SUPER SIDE KICKS

No Adults Allowed

PUFFIN

For Savannah

Chapter

I know this must have been hard for you.

But we're here because we're tired of being mistreated.

Tired of doing a thankless job.

Tired of being overshadowed and overworked.

He makes me clean his secret headquarters every day.

Wash his costume after every battle. *(Do you know how hard alien blood-stains are to scrub out?)*

And then he leaves me alone in his giant mansion while he's out taking all the credit!

8

Last week she got a parking ticket and went totally berserk.

She destroyed a skyscraper . . .

. . . and I almost got buried alive!

I never know when she's gonna snap. **It's just too stressful.**

Well, it's good to have you on board, Flygirl!

19

Chapter

What better way to celebrate our new team than with cookies? I baked them myself.

Oooh.

Delightful.

Aw, look, Goo's crying.

Goo so happy. Dr Enok **never** bake cookies.

We can use this old warehouse as our headquarters.

Though we'll have to do something about that hole in the roof.

OKAY, I GIVE UP! I GIVE UP!

I think I **peed** a little.

My handy justice belt is full of **crime-fighting gadgets.**

Smoke bombs, stun grenades, electronic trackers, lollipops, you name it.

34

Fighting crime with bugs?

That sounds pretty weak if you ask me.

I mean, with all due respect to Flygirl, how on earth are **teeny-tiny bugs** going to stop a super criminal?

I just don't think it's very . . .

. . . effective.

AAAAAAAAAAAAAAAAAAHHHHHHHH!

Very effective.

GET IT OFF!
GET IT OFF!

I stand corrected, Flygirl. I'll **never** pick a fight with you again.

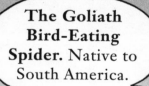

The Goliath Bird-Eating Spider. Native to South America.

While its venom is relatively harmless, it does pack a nasty bite.

They're the largest spiders in the world. And also the **cutest** if you ask me.

Back into your ball, little fella.

That thing is so gross.

What about you, Goo? You've already shown us how formidable you are, but **what exactly** are your powers?

Goo nervous. Goo never audition for super team before.

Don't be nervous, mate. You can be yourself around us.

Whatever Goo feel like, Goo do. Not think much about it.

I don't think you know how powerful you are, buddy.

Goo just happy to be here. With friends.

Dinomite turn now?

Hey, where is Dinomite?

This is so nice. Just being able to relax and not worry about Rampagin' Rita dropping a building on me.

I know, it's great without Captain Perfect being around to force me to –

JUNIOR JUSTICE!

Oh no.

Chapter

Thank goodness I found you, Junior Justice! I need you back at the mansion **right now**.

My laundry needs to be done and Super Mutt hasn't been taken for a walk yet.

Didn't you get the letter I left you?

Letter? I normally get **you** to read my fan mail.

Hee hee, ha ha, hoo hoo. Good one, Junior Justice.

Wait, you're serious?

Very.

But who's gonna wash my clothes, cook my food, clean my headquarters, cut my toenails and scrub my toilet?

It's always about **you**, isn't it?

Of course!

I'm Captain Perfect, the most **beloved person in the world,** after all.

49

Look, this was a nice little stunt, kids, but I've had enough of this nonsense.

C'mon, Junior Justice, let's go home.

Don't you get it, Captain? **We're not going back, ever!**

Why don't we discuss this after you've cooked me a nice . . .

Hmm, that's strange.

Pink's a weird colour for a warehouse wall. And the paint's still wet.

Captain Perfect, that not paint . . .

53

Where's Dr Enok hiding, **scumbag?**

Aaaah! Slippery devil!

Move! I've got my blaster set to vaporize!

No, stop attacking!

– leave.

Suddenly very sleepy . . .

Night-night time.

FHOOF!

Dinomite!

He's out cold.

I have to say, my feelings are hurt.

What have you done to Dinomite?

Oh, that? Just a new tranquillizer recipe I devised. Glad to see it can stop a full-grown **Tyrannosaurus rex**.

I don't know what you're up to, Enok, but I won't let you fly out of here in one piece.

Relax, Captain, I seek no violence with you and your playmates today.

I've just come to take back what is rightfully **mine**.

I speak, of course, of my beloved pet, Goo.

Please protect Goo. Please protect Goo.

60

ZKKKK

...you're in over your head.

ZAP!

GOO!

WHOOSH!

It was my fault for letting you escape, my pet. My containment device wasn't strong enough.

I won't be making that mistake again.

GLOOP!

Look, this new-found friendship is all very **touching**. But my patience is starting to wear thin.

Goo, it's time to return to the lab and –

What the?

OW!

Chapter

You know the best thing about our team?

What's that?

No adults allowed.

BYE!

79

Maybe Captain Perfect is **right.**
Maybe we're not cut out to make it on our own.
Maybe we're better off just being sidekicks.

What are
you talking
about?

We haven't even been
a team for **one day** and we've
already had our **headquarters
destroyed** and let one of our
members get **kidnapped.**

Just a minor
hiccup, chum. Nothing
we can't figure out.

**We don't
even have a team
name yet!**

We can worry about that later. We've got our **first mission to complete.**

Huh? What do you mean?

RESCUE GOO, OF COURSE!

Rescue Goo?

Goo's our mate, and we **never, ever leave a mate behind.** He risked his life to escape Dr Enok and now he's his prisoner again.

Who knows what that evil maniac is doing to him!

Yes, I agree.

Dr Enok is the **world's greatest criminal,** with an army of robot drones at his command.

I don't know if we can beat him.

Quit doubting yourself, JJ. We wouldn't have joined your team if we didn't believe in you.

But we don't even know where Enok is.

The location of his laboratory is a complete mystery.

Junior Justice, allow me to interrupt.

I went to the trouble of placing a tracker on Dr Enok in the middle of our altercation.

I'm getting a signal on his whereabouts. A remote island approximately 143 kilometres south-east from here.

Oh, sweet Ada, **I could kiss you!**

You really think we can do this?

It's what mates do for each other!

We owe it to Goo to give it a jolly good try.

Chapter

By leaving me to join those . . . those . . . I can barely say the word: **'heroes'**.

I'm afraid I can't let that go unpunished.

600 VOLTS

ZZZZZZKKKK!

AAAAH!

Goo sorry! Goo sorry! **Master no shock Goo!**

Do you promise to never leave me again?

Yes. Yes. **Goo promise!**

Mmmm, I'm not convinced.

1000 VOLTS

ZZZZZZZKKK!

I've always wondered how much electric voltage you can withstand before your molecules get **ripped apart.**

1000 volts seems close to your limit.

Gck gck tch.

1257 VOLTS

But you know what? I designed you to be **durable.**

1789 VOLTS

There it is! Dr Enok's lab.

Let's hope we're not too late.

We would have got here sooner if Dinomite hadn't stopped for **fish and chips.**

I don't like to fight super villains on an empty stomach.

So what's the plan, JJ?

Flygirl, see if you can find a way in from the roof. Once you get inside, you look for Goo.

This air vent looks like it leads down to the lab. But gee, it looks pretty gross in there.

Ah, quit complaining, girl. **Goo needs you!**

Nice of Dr Enok to throw us a party celebrating the return of his precious pet.

Not sure about his choice of music though.

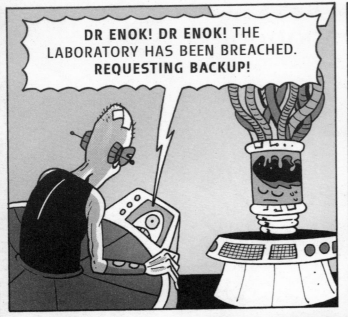

Goo, wake up! **WAKE UP!**

Oh, mate, you don't look so good.

Don't worry, I'm going to get you out of there.

These **Trap-Jaw Ants** have some of the most **powerful pincers** in the animal kingdom.

They should be able to burrow into the computer circuitry . . .

. . . and bite through the electrical cables.

105

Do you truly think you're going to survive out in the real world **without me to protect you?**

I dreamt you into existence. Created you out of nothing **but my own genius.**

YOU ARE A PART OF ME!

Do you think these children know you **like I know you?**

Care about you **like I care about you?**

Love you **like I love you?**

SLOOP!

Goo?

NO.

MORE.

Uh-oh.

GOO!

Well, chum . . .

. . . remind me to **never** make you angry.

Goo cannot believe friends come for him.

You're a part of the team, remember?

Yeah, mates don't leave each other behind.

So happy. **Goo cry now.**

Chapter

Fine.

Listen, we and the rest of the superhero community heard what happened. That you defeated Dr Enok and his robot army.

Your hair . . . it seems to defy gravity. Can I take a sample for analysis?

Sorry, friend. Under no circumstances does anyone touch my perfect hair.

Heck, dudes, we heard you even destroyed Enok's lab.

GOOD BASHING!

We can't take credit for destroying the lab. That was all Goo.

Are you ready to believe he's a good guy now?

Yes, we're willing to accept that young Goo is on our side now.

But I'll be keeping a very close eye on him.

And, look, we're sorry about the way things ended back in the warehouse. We should have had more faith in you and your abilities.

Is there anything we can do to make it up to you? Maybe buy you some pizza?

I can teach you how to blast things!

Rita bash something for you?

And so, a few days later . . .

Huff puff.

Okay, this is the last of the scrap metal from Dr Enok's lab.

Where should I put it?

Just follow Ada's directions. She'll show you where to place everything.

Materials for top exterior walls and windows. Proceed to *27th floor.*

Awesome, a training room to practise martial arts!

And a room for all my bugs!

This is my library, filled with the complete works of the greatest writers and thinkers in history.

All first editions, I might add.

To be continued . . .

GAVIN AUNG THAN

SUPER SIDE KICKS

Ocean's Revenge

The Super Sidekicks will return in their next amazing adventure!

The Queen of the Seas is sick of humans using the oceans as a junkyard, so she decides to give the land-dwellers a taste of their own medicine. Giant plastic trash monsters, mythical sea creatures and killer crabs attack in . . .

SUPER SIDEKICKS BOOK TWO:
Ocean's Revenge

GAVIN AUNG THAN always dreamt of being a superhero when he was a kid. Now he's doing the next best thing, writing and drawing the adventures of the Super Sidekicks! If he could choose, he would have the fighting ability of JJ, the brains of Dinomite, the flexibility of Goo, be able to fly like Flygirl and, above all, have hair as beautiful as Captain Perfect.

You can visit Gav's website at
www.aungthan.com